Dropping In C

SAUDI ARABIA

Patricia M. Moritz

A Geography Series

ROURKE CORPORATION, INC.
VERO BEACH, FLORIDA 32964

Printed in the United States of America

Revised Edition 2004

Library of Congress
Cataloging-In-Publication Data

Moritz, Patricia M.
Saudi Arabia/Patricia M. Moritz.
p. cm. — (Dropping in on)
Includes bibliographical references (p.) and index.
Summary: Briefly describes some of the major cities of Saudi Arabia, as well as its foods, religion, and art of calligraphy.
ISBN 0-86593-494-0
1. Saudi Arabia—Juvenile literature.
[1.Saudi Arabia—Description and travel.] I. Title.
II. Series.
DS204.M67 1998
953.8—dc21   98-15230
                                            CIP
                                            AC

Saudi Arabia
■ ■ ■ ■ ■ ■ ■ ■ ■ ■ ■ ■ ■ ■

Official Name: Kingdom of Saudi Arabia

Area: 756,981 square miles

Population: 26,417,599

Capital: Riyadh

Largest City: Riyadh (3,724,100)

Highest Elevation:
Jabal Sawda' (10,278 feet)

Official Language: Arabic

Major Religion: Muslim

Money: Saudi riyal

Form of Government:
Absolute monarchy

Flag:

TABLE OF CONTENTS

Our Blue Ball—The Earth

The Earth can be divided into two hemispheres. The word hemisphere means "half a ball"—in this case, the ball is the Earth.

The equator is an imaginary line that runs around the middle of the Earth. It separates the Northern Hemisphere from the Southern Hemisphere. North America—where Canada, the United States, and Mexico are located—is in the Northern Hemisphere.

The Northern Hemisphere

When the North Pole is tilted toward the sun, the sun's most powerful rays strike the northern half of the Earth and less sunshine hits the Southern Hemisphere. That is when people in the Northern Hemisphere enjoy summer. When the

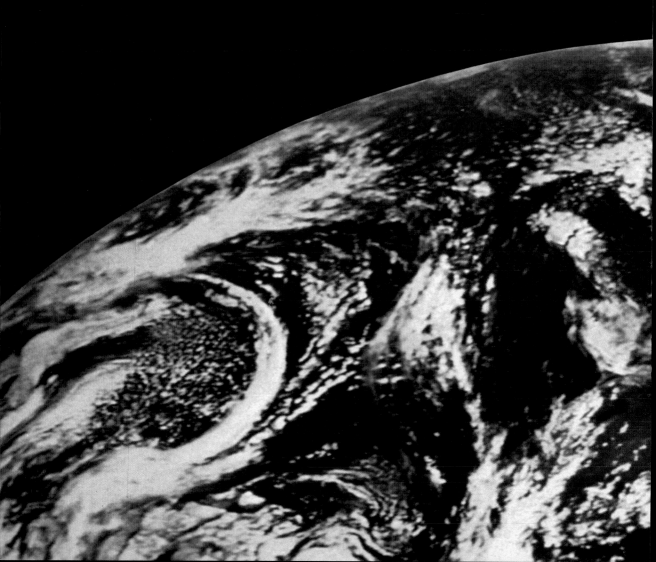

North Pole is tilted away from the sun, and the Southern Hemisphere receives the most sunshine, the seasons reverse. Then winter comes to the Northern Hemisphere. Seasons in the Northern Hemisphere and the Southern Hemisphere are always opposite.

Get Ready for Saudi Arabia

Let's take a trip! Climb into your hot-air balloon, and we'll drop in on a country that lies at the crossroads of three continents: Europe, Asia, and Africa. Saudi Arabia is the largest Arab country. It is a modern, technologically advanced nation with an ancient history. Saudi Arabia is a monarchy, ruled by a king and an appointed council of ministers.

Climate in Saudi Arabia varies from more than 100 degrees F. in summer to below freezing in winter in the north and central regions. The southeast part of the country is known as the "Empty Quarter," and is the largest sand desert on earth.

Saudi Arabia is the spiritual center for the Islamic religion. The followers of Islam are called Muslims. They believe in one god named Allah. The holiest cities in the Islamic religion are located in Saudi Arabia. Muslims from all over the world make a pilgrimage, or *haj*, to these holy cities.

Only Muslim pilgrims, businesspeople, and foreign workers are permitted to enter the Kingdom of Saudi Arabia.

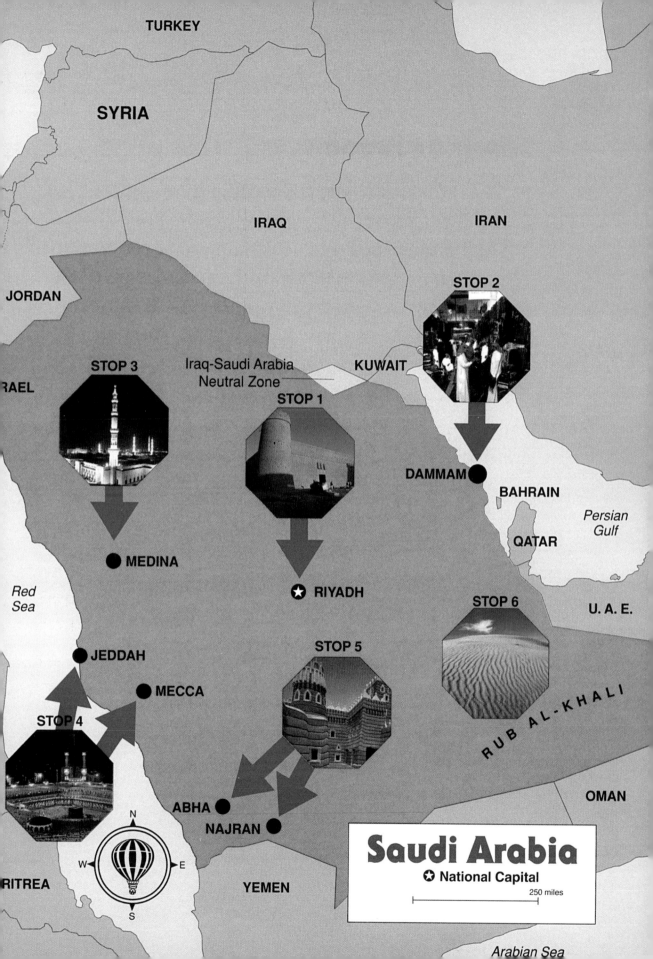

Stop 1: Riyadh

The city of Riyadh is located in an oasis almost in the center of the country. It is the capital of Saudi Arabia and a major commercial center. Until recently, Riyadh was one of the most isolated and least-known cities in the world.

In the city you will see clay forts and palaces amid modern high-rise buildings. The traditional *souks*, or bazaars, are in the center of the city. Here you can buy anything from gold to decorative coffee pots.

Among the most interesting places to visit are the King's Palace, the many mosques, and Saudi Arabia's first museum—the Museum of Archaeology and Ethnology.

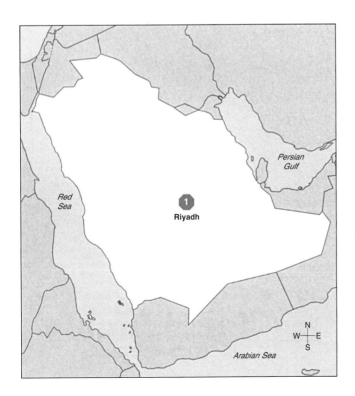

Opposite: Al Masmaq Fort in Riyadh.

 *Now let's fly **northeast** to Dammam.*

The Monarchy

The founder of modern Arabia was Ibn Saud. After 22 years of tribal warfare, he united the four main regions of the country. In 1932, as King Abdul Aziz Ibn Saud, he proclaimed the new Kingdom of Saudi Arabia. The present ruler is King Abdullah bin Abdulaziz al-Saud. He is the fifth of Ibn Saud's sons to govern the country. The king is chosen by the princes of the royal family. There are about 5,000 princes in the royal family. Many of them hold important political offices.

Until 1992, the country was ruled entirely by the king. Today the king appoints a council of ministers, or cabinet, to help him form and implement policies. The king is also prime minister and owns all the undistributed land in the country.

The Kingdom has one of the most strict Muslim societies in the world. The king governs according to the rules of Islam, called Shari'a. He acts as the country's highest court of appeal. The royal family protects the holy sites of Mecca and Medina out of a deep sense of responsibility toward Islam. It is a top priority to

Pictured above is king Abdullah, king of Saudi Arabia.

the Kingdom's leaders to provide safety, security, and comfort to pilgrims and visitors.

Stop 2: Dammam

The city of Dammam is located on the coast of the Persian Gulf in the eastern part of the country. Oil fields located in this region are the source of nearly all the country's wealth. Dammam is Saudi Arabia's second most important port after Jeddah.

Here you can see the King Fahd Bridge, the second longest bridge in the world. This famous bridge links the Kingdoms of Saudi Arabia and Bahrain.

In the center of Dammam, you can visit the traditional bazaars and shisha, or pipe-smoking houses. The main bazaar, called the Souk al-Hareem, sells everything from food to gold and antiques. You might see some veiled women here selling cloth. Outside of the bazaar, you almost never see women in public.

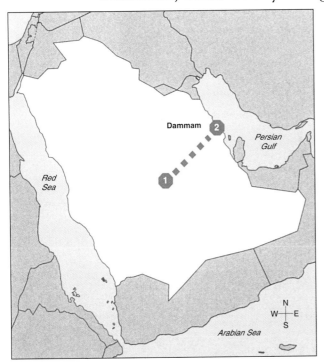

Opposite: Traditional carpets being sold in the bazaar, or souk.

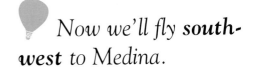 *Now we'll fly south-west to Medina.*

Stop 3: Medina

The city of Medina is located in the central western part of the country. It is the country's second holiest city and lies just north of the holiest one, Mecca.

More than a thousand years ago, the prophet Muhammed, the founder of Islam, began his teaching here after fleeing religious persecution in his birthplace of Mecca.

One of the most interesting features of Medina is that the entire city is surrounded by double walls with nine gates.

In the city's main mosque you can visit the tombs of Muhammed, his daughter Fatima, and the caliph Omar. Devout Muslims try to make the *haj*, or pilgrimage, to Medina at least once in their lifetime.

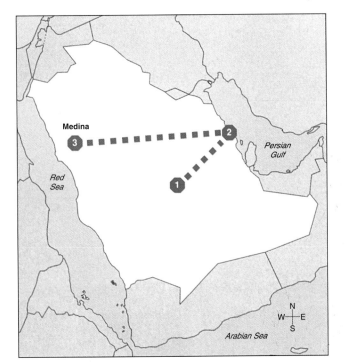

Opposite: The Prophet's Mosque in Medina.

Now let's fly **southward** to Jeddah and Mecca.

Growing Up in Saudi Arabia

In Saudi Arabia, a family is often composed of parents and children living communally with other relatives.

The kingdom provides free education for all boys and girls. However, the government does not require children to go to school. Children begin primary school at age six. Many do not continue their education past age twelve. Boys and girls are educated in separate schools. Because of the traditional roles for women in this society, more boys than girls attend school.

The government has set up youth programs so that free time is spent in a useful way and special talents can be developed. Sports are widely encouraged. There are many stadiums and sports centers. Soccer is the favorite sport here. One of the most interesting pastimes is camel racing.

Opposite: Camel racing is a popular sport in Saudi Arabia.

Stop 4: Jeddah and Mecca

Jeddah is the second largest city in the kingdom, and the major port on the Red Sea. It is the starting point for pilgrims to Mecca and Medina.

The Corniche is the main highway in Jeddah which runs beside the Red Sea. Along the Corniche, you will see high-rise office buildings and sculptures by many internationally known artists. In the old city you can see traditional coral-faced houses with wooden balconies.

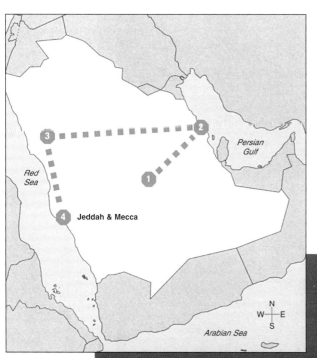

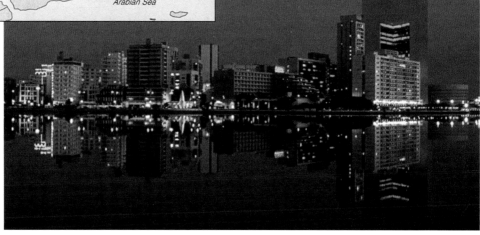

Above: The skyline of Jeddah.

Above: The Great Mosque.

The holy city of Mecca is just east of Jeddah. This walled city is located in a narrow valley surrounded by hills and castles. Mecca was the birthplace of Muhammed, the founder of Islam, and is the country's holiest city. All Muslims try to make the *haj*, or pilgrimage, to Mecca at least once in their lifetime. The Great Mosque, containing the Black Stone, is located here. No matter where in the world they may be, Muslims face the direction of Mecca and the Black Stone when praying. Non-Muslims are forbidden to enter the city, and any caught within its walls face serious punishment.

 *Now let's fly **southeast** to Abha and Najran.*

Islamic Calligraphy

Calligraphy is the basic Islamic art form and is very respected in Saudi Arabia. Historically, the primary subject matter for calligraphy has been the Koran, the holy book of the Islamic faith.

Showing human forms has generally been avoided in Islamic art, because of a fear that it may lead to hero or saint worship. Throughout Saudi Arabia, calligraphy is the main theme in metal work, ceramics, glass, textiles, painting, and sculpture. Inscriptions can be found on the interior walls of mosques, as well as public and private office buildings and homes.

Museums in Saudi Arabia collect and display rare manuscripts. Many organizations commission works of calligraphy and provide training in this art form.

Opposite: The cloth that covers the Holy Kaaba at the Great Mosque in Mecca.

Stop 5: Abha and Najran

The cities of Abha and Najran are located in the southwest corner of the country. Set in the Asir Mountains, Abha enjoys a temperate climate with light summer rains and winter mists. It is one of the most picturesque places in Saudi Arabia and is a popular holiday resort and tourist attraction.

Najran is located in an oasis, just east of Abha. An unusual feature of this town is the numerous mud houses. They are five- to eight-stories tall. Some of these mud houses have stained-glass windows. Many important archaeological sites are found in this region, such as the palace of the former emirs, or rulers, in the Najran Valley.

Photo: An old palace in Najran.

*Now let's fly **east** to Rub al-Khali.*

Stop 6: Rub al-Khali

In the southeast area of the country is the Rub al-Khali, known as the "Empty Quarter." Its southern boundaries with Yemen and Oman are not clearly defined.

The Rub al-Khali is the largest continuous sand desert on earth. It is one of the world's most dry and hostile deserts. It has no water, is uninhabited, and is almost featureless. Large areas of the desert even remain unexplored! This desert has some of the largest sand dunes anywhere—some as tall as 984 feet high. That is more than twice as tall as the Great Pyramid in Egypt!

 Now it's time to set sail for home.

Persian
Gulf

Red
Sea

3 ······· 2

1

4 ······· 6 Rub Al-Khali

5

N
W——E
S

Arabian Sea

The Foods of Saudi Arabia

The cuisine in Saudi Arabia has been influenced by immigrants from all over the Arab world. Meat and rice are the staples of their diet. Usually dishes are made with mutton, chicken, goat, or camel. The meat may be stuffed with rice, nuts, and herbs and served on a large bed of rice.

An interesting fact is the way in which the Saudi people eat. Families and guests alike eat from a communal dish using the fingers of the right hand only. Soup or salad is often served alongside the main course, and *shami* or *samul* bread is eaten with every meal. In the coastal regions more fish is served.

Dates are traditional for dessert. There is also a milk pudding called *muhallabiyah*, and a favorite honey- and nut-filled pastry called *bakhlava*.

29

Glossary

calligraphy   Beautiful handwriting, which in Saudi Arabia is used as a decorative element.

Islam   The Muslim religion which believes in one god, Allah, and the founder and prophet Muhammed.

Koran   The holy book of the Islamic religion.

mosque   A Muslim place of worship.

Muslim   A true believer and follower of the religion of Islam.

nomads   A group or tribe that moves from place to place, rather than living in permanent homes.

oasis   An area in a desert that has enough water for trees and crops to grow.

souk   An open-air marketplace or bazaar.

Further Reading

Reed, Jennifer Bond. *Saudi Royal Family*. Chelsea House, 2003.

Deady, Kathleen W. *Saudi Arabia: A Question and Answer Book*. Capstone Press, 2005.

Temple, Bob. *Saudi Arabia*. Childs World, 2001.

Italia, Bob. *Saudi Arabia*. Abdo Publishing, 2003.

Suggested Web Sites

www.saudinf.com/

www.saudiembassy.net

www.hejleh.com/countries/saudi.html

Index

Acknowledgments and Photo Credits
Cover: © PNI; pp. 11, 13, 15, 17, 19, 20, 21, 23, 24–25: Courtesy Kingdom of Saudi Arabia, Ministry of Information; pp. 26–27: © PhotoDisc; pg. 29: © PNI.
Maps by Paul Calderon.